The Secret Baseball Challenge

The Secret
Baseball Challenge

by

Jerry B. Jenkins

MOODY PRESS

CHICAGO

This Guideposts edition is published by special
arrangement with Moody Press

ISBN: 0-8024-8232-5

14 15 16 Printing/LC/Year 95 94 93 92 91

Printed in the United States of America

To you, yes you, the one with the dream

Contents

1

Last Summer

I never dreamed that last summer would be the best one of my life. Not at all. My dad's work as a road construction boss took him to Michigan, and we didn' t see him for almost three months. My two little sisters, Amy and Jennifer, had to go with my mother on her babysitting job.

What a babysitting job! She had to get the girls up early and leave for Chicago before I was even out of bed. For the whole summer she babysat for some rich people's baby from six in the morning until six at night, Monday through Saturday.

She and Dad had spent a lot of hours talking about whether she should even take the job and what they were going to do with me if she did. Right up until the last week before she finally took the job, I thought I would have to go with her every day.

That was Dad's idea. He didn't get to play much when he was a kid, and he thought it would "do the boy some good" if I went with Mom and helped watch my sisters while she took care of the rich kid and did all the housework.

Well, Mom felt bad enough about having to take such a horrible job, but we needed the money and she couldn't talk the rich people into letting their baby boy stay at our place in the country.

I wanted to argue, to plead and beg to be able to stay

alone at home during the day, and I had all the reasons dreamed up too. But that's not how anybody talks to my dad. He doesn't get talked into things. He just decides, that's all.

Actually, I think it was Mom who helped him decide on this one. She set up all the rules and asked Dad if we could try it for the first two weeks.

"He just turned twelve, Bev," my dad reminded her. "He's not ready to be left out here all by himself all day for the summer."

Mom stood and moved to the window, staring out at our small farm. "I'll make him call me twice a day, and he'll have chores. He'll have to weed the garden, pick the vegetables, do the yardwork, and keep the place up. And there would be limits on where he can go. Mrs. Ferguson said he could tell her any time he goes anywhere so I'd know how to reach him if I ever had to."

My dad didn't look convinced, and I was sure he'd never allow it. "What's he going to do for meals?"

I wanted to answer, to tell him that that was the least of my worries, but I knew it would just irritate him, and anyway, I wanted to know if Mom had thought of an answer to the food problem herself. She had.

"He can get his own breakfast. And I'll make up his lunches and put them in the freezer."

I was getting excited. I could see Dad softening. What a summer I was going to have! What freedom!

Mom continued. "Dallas, you know the rules. Your boundaries are Olive Street and Toboggan Road north and south, and the highway frontage road and Baker Street east and west."

To tell you the truth, I was shocked. That gave me about a mile square. It might not sound like much, but I was expecting a lot less. All my best friends lived within that area.

"When your chores are done, you may have friends over, and you can play in the barn or in the shed, but you can't

4

have more than one friend in the house with you at a time, and then for lunch only if they bring their own."

All of a sudden, it became clear to me that Mom and Dad had quit talking about it and had begun setting down the rules for me. It was all I could do to sit still. I wanted to call Jimmy Calabresi so bad, but I didn't want to show my excitement for fear the whole deal would fade away.

I don't think I fooled my dad, though, trying to take it all in stride. He was a kid once himself, and he knew. When they finally agreed that that was how it was going to be, that we would try leaving me at home during the day for the first couple of weeks of the summer, we ate dinner and then Dad asked me to take a walk with him.

Even when my dad was tired and troubled, which he was now, I liked to be around him. He was hard and tanned from working outdoors all his life, and I liked the way the summer sun kept his brown hair bleached almost yellow.

His boots made scuffing sounds in the dirt in our back acres, but unless I hurried I found myself behind him. He wore a white, sleeveless pullover shirt to work everyday and khaki pants that came right to the top of his boots.

I made the mistake once of telling him that short pants like that weren't cool. He just stared at me for the longest time and spoke quitely. "Worryin' about trippin' over your trouser cuffs when an earth mover's behind you ain't cool either. Not too many cool guys last long on the road, Dal."

I hated it when he started calling me Dal, and I told him so. I think he tried to quit. He said he didn't do it on purpose but that it was just what came out when he thought of me and how much he loved me.

I could tell it was hard for him to say that, but every once in a while he'd say it anyway. He wanted me to know I was special because I was his firstborn and his only boy. I guess I would've felt special whether he said it or not, because he was a good dad and everybody liked him.

When we we arrived at the corral he pointed to the top of the white fence, and I climbed it. I remember when I first

5

tried to sit on that rickety thing and how he laughed when I held on for dear life.

Now he sat across from me with the corner post between us. "You know why this corral's empty, Dal?"

I nodded. "Sure. 'Cause you sold Lightning."

"You loved that horse, didn't you, boy?"

I nodded, but I didn't say anything. I didn't want to cry. Dad had brought that horse home for me when he was a colt and I was five. He was chestnut brown but still I wanted to name him Silver like the Lone Ranger's white horse. That's what I called him the first night.

But there had been a storm. Lots of lightning and thunder. I begged Dad to let me go out to the stable and be with Silver, but he told me the horse would never get used to storms if we were always out there with him.

So, I just sat on the edge of my bed, watching the open window of the stable and seeing Silver look almost white every time the lightning flashed. I cried and cried that night, listening to him whinny and kick around.

I thought my dad was pretty mean then, but by the time the storm was over, Silver had quieted down. And I had come up with a new name for him. Young as I was, I still fed and groomed Lightning every day, walking him, riding him, everything.

Finally, I could speak without my voice breaking. "*You* loved him too, Dad."

He nodded. "Yeah." His voice was husky. "But not as much as you. You loved that horse like most boys love their dogs." He was right, and I hoped he wouldn't make me talk about it anymore. "I knew it would break your heart and that you'd never understand, and there's nothin' I want to do less than hurt my boy. Sellin' that beautiful animal was one of the hardest things I ever had to do in my life."

I looked deep into my dad's eyes. I knew some of the things he'd had to do that he didn't like, but I never figured he had them listed in order. If I wasn't so choked up, I would have asked him, but he saved me the trouble.

6

He frowned. "You probably think seein' my pa die when I was about your age was one of 'em."

I whispered. "Would have been for me."

"Well, believe it or not, there have been tougher ones. Not that I didn't love Pa. You know I did. Taught me so much. Was such a good Christian. I'm still trying to live so Pa would be proud of me."

There was one of those late spring breezes that made you shiver even though you could still see the sun full and low in the western sky. When my dad talked like this, I didn't know what to say, so I didn't say anything. Of couse, I was curious about those things he said were tougher for him than seeing his own father die when Dad was almost thirteen.

His father got tangled up in some kind of farm machinery, and Dad heard him calling for help. But there was nothing Dad could do but run for the neighbors, because if his father wasn't strong enough to free himself, a young boy sure wasn't either.

By the time Dad returned with help, his father was dead. It took almost all of my life to piece that together from the many times I'd heard the story. One thing I was sure of: Dad could never tell the whole story himself. It was too painful, and it didn't take a genius to know why.

He had a faraway look in his eye. "Losing my pa made me a better dad. At least I hope it did. All I want to be is a good dad, Dal. You know that. So, tough as it was, something good came of it. Who knows what kind of a person I might have turned out to be if I hadn't had the memory of my pa to keep me straight?"

I squinted into the orange sun and turned to face my dad. I had the feeling that if I asked him what could be tougher than losing his father, he might get out of the mood for talking. And I didn't want that.

I spoke carefully. "I hated when you sold Lightning."

Dad smiled. "Did you hate me?"

I didn't answer right away. He knew me pretty well. I had to admit it. "I wasn't too thrilled with you for a while."

He smiled. "You hated me. You wouldn't even look at me, let alone talk to me, for three days."

I shook my head. "I would never hate you, Dad. Even if I think you're wrong sometimes."

Dad put his hands on the top rail on either side of him and swung his legs back and down till he stood looking up at me. "Still think I had any other choice?"

I looked away. "Nope. I wish you could have had Grandma move in with us, but—"

"But it was impossible." He had spoken quickly. I had irritated him, or at least remembering his decision had upset him. From the corner of my eye I could tell he wasn't looking at me anymore.

"If there had been any way we could have handled her. . . . But I couldn't saddle your mother with that, with the kind of care Grandma needs. If I could take care of her myself, I would. But she's like a baby, Dallas. She can't do anything for herself. She needs professional care all day and all night."

I had this feeling that I should reach down and touch Dad's shoulder and tell him I knew, that I understood, and that it was all right. But I had never done anything like that before, and I couldn't bring myself to do it then.

Dad folded his hands in front of him and sighed. "Putting her in that home, as wonderful as it is, was one of those hardest things I've ever had to do, Dal. They tell me that she doesn't recognize me anymore anyway, that she doesn't know who put her in there and won't hold any grudges as if she'd been abandoned.

"And I know it's true. But I'd still like to know how come she cries when we visit her and cries even harder when we leave." He thought a long while and pawed at the ground with the toe of his boot. "Only one other thing was hard as havin' to do that."

Dad didn't seem to want to talk anymore. Bugs started biting, and it was getting darker, but I would have sat out there with him all night just to find out what the other toughest thing was that he had to do. Tougher even than seeing his own pa die.

8

2
Dad's Advice

Dad reached up and let me slide down off the corral fence into his arms. With my feet still high in the air, he swung me to the ground. We walked deep into the acres toward the setting sun.

Finally, he spoke again. "Today, tonight, this afternoon, right now. This is one of those tough things."

I didn't know what he meant, so I just waited. I knew once he got started talking—which was rare—he'd finish.

When he stopped to sit in the tall grass, we were in the deep shadows of the trees along the back end of our property. Dad pulled his feet up under him and wrapped his hands around his knees.

"I put your grandma in a home because I couldn't see any other way. Way I was raised, kids took care of their ma and pa till they died. No question. Well, I'm still takin' care of her, but it's just by payin' the bill and visiting her when we can. You know, Dal, I probably shoulda told you this when I sold your horse, but that home for Grandma costs me more than half of my paycheck every month."

I nodded. The truth was, he *had* told me that, but I had been crying over my horse and didn't want to hear it. Later, my mom showed me on paper how all of one of my dad's two paychecks every month had to be put aside for the nursing home bill, and part of the other paycheck too.

She also reminded me that my horse wasn't the only thing Dad sold. He had also got rid of our station wagon, leaving us with only his old pickup. When Mom needed it, he had to find a ride to work. He also sold the rest of the livestock at real low prices and auctioned off all his old farm equipment, some of which had belonged to his father once.

Mom wouldn't let me blame him. "He's working road construction for us. All he ever wanted to do was farm, and now he can't even play at it after work."

After that I quit moping around about Lightning in front of my dad, and I started being nice to him again. I felt bad about the way I had acted, but I never apologized. I wanted to now, but even more, I wanted to listen.

Dad cleared his throat. "I didn't get a whole lot of money for Lightning. At least not what he was worth. But that first payment at the nursing home was a whopper, and we still had to eat and pay the mortgage."

I nodded again.

"Well, Dal, I gotta follow this federal job to Michigan for the summer. I hate to do it, but I know it's right. And your mom needs this babysittin' job too. If the pickup holds out, she'll be able to get back and forth."

He quit talking for a while and hid his face in his hands. He wasn't crying, but he might as well have been. I was cold and getting tired, and in a selfish way I hoped we'd get back into the house in time for me to call Jimmy before he went to bed.

Dad took a deep breath and looked up, and I knew he was a lot more tired than I was. "This kills me. Leaving you here alone over the summer."

"It's all right, Dad, really. I'm looking forward to it."

"Of course you are. I know that. Most any kid would. But is it the best thing for you? There's no way. Coopin' you up in some rich guy's house is no good either. I wish I could take you with me to Michigan."

I was stunned. Did he mean it? That would be even better than spending the summer alone with my friends.

I couldn't even speak, but Dad could see in my eyes that

12

I was getting my hopes up. He reacted quickly. "Forget it, Dallas. It's impossible. I'm staying with a bunch of men in a dormitory, and there would be nothing for you to do all day. I'd be more ashamed of myself for doing that to you than making you stay here."

"Don't feel ashamed, Dad. I'll be all right here."

Dad drew circles in the dirt with his large, hard fingers. The sky was pink and purple, and I could hardly see the ground. "There's three things I want you to do for me, Dallas. You know how you like to be the one readin' the devotional book at the table every night and we always let Amy read from her *Living Bible*?"

I nodded.

"Well, I want you to do that every morning on your own. Read the devotional and your Bible. And you'll pray for me, won't you?"

I nodded again.

"Then, when your mother gets home, you won't be eatin' with the rest of the family unless she makes you up a snack or somethin'. All their meals will be at the other place. So you got to read the devotional out loud for the girls and help Mom get 'em to bed. OK?"

That sounded easy enough. But he said there were three things. "I also want you to be careful, Dal. You know everybody around here, so you keep an eye out for strangers. You don't have to lie to anybody to keep from lettin' on that your mom and dad aren't home. It's none of anybody's business. You keep doors locked, you stay in the boundaries your mom set for ya, and you use your head. Understand?"

"Uh-huh."

"Now, Dal, there's one more thing, and this is somethin' you can do for me that will make me feel a little better about leavin' you here this summer. No one will ever know but you whether you do it or not, but it's a way you can train yourself for later in life.

"I want you to decide from the beginning that you're gonna get all your work done before you play. No callin'

13

Jimmy, no ridin' around on your bike, no playin' ball, no dallyin', no nothin' till all your chores are done. Might take ya coupla hours a day, but you do 'em first thing. Hear?"

That was one I didn't want to hear, but I didn't want to pretend to agree and then not do it either. I didn't answer, but Dad wouldn't let up. "Will you do that for me, Dal?"

I shrugged.

"How about it?"

"I guess, if I have to."

"You have to. I really want you to. And like I say, there's nobody gonna know if you don't do it that way, 'cept you. But I want you to promise me you'll do that."

"But Dad, that's how you work, and you never wind up with any time to play."

"Hey, we play a lot!"

It was true. When he got home from work we played catch every night. But I always felt guilty about it because I wanted to play longer and he always seemed so stiff and tired. I could tell I had hurt his feelings, and in trying to make up for that, I agreed. "OK, Dad."

"Good, Dal. You'll be glad you did that. Now I've got some bad news for you."

My stomach flip-flopped. "Bad news?"

"I don't want you watchin' any television unless your mom is home."

I couldn't believe it. "No television!? You're kidding!"

"Nope. That's my rule. Might's well unplug it, because your mom probably won't let you watch when she gets home either."

"Man, Dad! What about ball games?"

"No, sir. I'm sorry. I don't want you wastin' two, three hours of sunshine every day to sit in front of the TV. That'll be good for you too, Dal, and you won't be tempted to watch all day."

"I wouldn't!"

"You might."

He was right, I knew. I had watched lots of junk on television when I had to stay home from school a couple of

14

times. I wasn't going to agree or nod on this one. I'd obey if he made me, but I wasn't going to pretend to like it.

"I don't want you watchin' at the other guys' houses either, understand?"

I nodded miserably. My days had been scheduled for me. I had to read my Bible and the devotional book and then get my breakfast, do all my chores, and then find things to do all day, anything and everything except watch TV.

"I'm not askin' you on this one, Dal. I'm tellin' you, OK?"

It wasn't OK, but what was I supposed to say? "I guess."

"I'll call you every second or third night, but I won't be checkin' up on ya. I'll never ask if you're doin' what I'm tellin' ya, Dallas, because you're old enough now to know to do what's right. I'm countin' on ya."

That's what I was afraid of. Now I'd really have to do it. Somehow, when Dad put it to me that way, he always got me to do what he said. If I didn't, I felt so bad that I had to admit it to him, and that was worse. It made me feel better after that, but worrying about it and dreading the time when I would have to tell him was never worth it.

I still didn't like it, and I didn't agree that this was the best thing for me. But I did know that he loved me and that he thought he was doing what was best for me. And I didn't know how I could ask for more than that. He thought all this work and discipline would make a man out of me. We'd have to see.

3
The First Day

A few weeks later, school was out, my father had left for Michigan with tearful good-byes all around, and I had told Jimmy Calabresi all about my staying home alone all summer.

After church the night before she began her babysitting job, Mom gave me last minute instructions, reminding me of everything she had been telling me for days. "You won't be up when I leave, because the girls and I will have to leave here by five-thirty, but you'll want to be up at least by eight to get everything done."

That was a laugh. I had so many plans that I would be up no later than seven. The one thing I hadn't counted on was how much I would miss Amy and Jennifer and how little time I would get to spend with them. Since they had to be up around five to be ready to go with my mother at five-thirty, she would be putting them to bed almost as soon as she got home around five-thirty in the evening. They also took naps at the rich people's home, the Blasingames.

My eyes popped open early the next morning when I heard my mother padding around the house, getting the girls ready. I smelled instant coffee, which was the only thing she would take time for before heading off to the Blasingames' to prepare their breakfasts. They begged her to just move in with them for the summer, but she refused.

I peeked out the window when I heard my mother slam the front doors of the pickup. Each had to be slammed hard at least three times before it would catch and she could lock it. I smiled at the stories my father always told about how the people in the city complained when he would slam his door so many times every morning. That was one good thing about living in the country now. Nobody but the animals knew or cared how loud the pickup was.

I pulled the shade against the harsh early morning sun and tumbled back into bed, hands behind my head. Within minutes my body was limp again, but the dreams of all my plans and the nervousness about suddenly being alone in the big, old farm house kept me on edge, even in my sleep.

I heard noises I had never noticed before and found I could look forward to my mother and sisters being home before dark every night. Already I missed them, and that made me smile with surprise. I rolled over and drew my knees up. The morning was cool, perfect for another hour of sleep.

Suddenly I heard a smack against my window, as if a bird or small stone had hit it. I jumped but didn't open my eyes. A couple of seconds later, what seemed like two or three small rocks hit the window at the same time.

I bolted from my bed and yanked back the curtains. The culprit was bending over, gathering more cinders from the driveway to toss up at the window. I nearly scared the life out of him by throwing up the window and screaming at him. "Calabresi! What do you think you're doing! You wanna break my window?"

Jimmy Calabresi, a little shorter and stockier than me, with black hair and brown eyes and olive skin, fell on his seat at the first shout. He frowned and stared up at me, then broke into his trademark grin, mouth full of gleaming teeth that even made a summer morning look brighter.

"C'mon, man! It's almost seven o'clock already, and you've got no parents here. Let's do somethin'!"

"I'll be right down."

Jimmy was swinging in the glider on the porch when I

barefooted my way out there. My hair stood on end, and I wore only my pajama bottoms. Calabresi, sitting there with his arms folded, just shook his head at me. "Man, you're not even dressed yet! I wake you up?"

"Nah. I'm still sleepin'."

Jimmy laughed. "That's funny, but man, the summer's wastin' away. Let's do somethin'."

"Like what?"

"Like anything. Where does your dad stash his dirty magazines?"

"You know better than that!"

"Oh, yeah. Your dad doesn't have any. You wanna see my dad's? He keeps 'em in a locked cabinet in his den downstairs, and he doesn't think I know where he keeps the key. We can pretend to play pool or something and get in there. My ma's goin' shoppin' this afternoon."

"Forget it. I don't want to do that."

"Why not? Maybe he's got some new ones."

"Makes me feel too guilty. I'd wind up having to tell my mom or dad."

Jimmy shook his head and frowned. "What a baby!"

"If you think I'm a baby, what do you wanna play with me for?"

" 'Cause you're my best friend. Even if you are weird."

"Thanks."

Jimmy ignored my sarcasm. "So, what're you gonna do, sit around all morning?"

"No, I've got a whole list. I was just about to get up."

Jimmy clapped. "All right! What's first?"

"You mean you really wanna do what I'm gonna do? I don't figure on being free to play until about nine."

"Nine? What in the world do you have to do? And who's gonna know if you play first and do your work a couple of hours before your ma gets back?"

"I'll know."

"You amaze me, O'Neil. C'mon!"

"No. I've got my list, and I was the one who wrote it up.

I'll tell you what it is only if you agree in advance to do everything with me. Otherwise, I'll see you at nine."

Jimmy stood as if to leave and walked to the edge of the porch, his back to me. His hands were thrust deep into the pockets of his shorts. For a minute I thought he'd leave and not come back at all. But we'd been through too much. I had never been able to get him to come to church, but he had never been able to get me to do things I shouldn't. At least not too much.

Jimmy could be stubborn. I turned and headed back into the house. He turned. "All right, let me see the list."

"No, you know the deal. You guarantee first that you'll do everything with me. Then I show you the list."

"All right! OK! Let's see it."

I motioned for him to follow me into the house. I had left the list on the dining room table. He read it. "Breakfast first. Good. I've already eaten, but I can eat again."

"Sorry, my mom said anybody who eats with me here has to bring his own."

But Jimmy wasn't listening. He had read further.

"Oh, no! Reading and prayer? I'm not prayin'!"

"Don't worry. I'll pray. And I'll read too, but you gotta listen."

"And you're mowin' the lawn up to the barn after that? Man, that's more'n an acre!"

"It's two."

"Forget it. I want out of the deal. Call me when you're finished."

"Then we're not best friends anymore, Jimmy." I hated to have to be like that with him, but sometimes it was the only thing that convinced him.

He shrugged and sighed. "All right, but get on with it."

While I ate, he sat with the cereal box in his lap. He reached deep inside it. "You think your mother would mind if your best friend in the world took one bite of dry cereal?"

I shook my head, knowing he would hate it without sugar anyway. He gobbled down a huge mouthful just to be

20

cantankerous, and then, of course, he wanted a swig of milk or orange juice. "There's plenty of water. My mother measures the milk and orange juice cartons to see how much I've had."

He headed for the sink and a couple of swallows of water. "You're kiddin'. She *measures* the cartons?"

"Course I'm kiddin', you idiot! What kind of a mother would do that?"

He left the dirty glass on the counter. You-know-who would be washing it after dinner, but I figured I was putting him through enough grief without making him do it.

I got my devotional booklet and Bible from the top of the refrigerator.

He turned up his nose and scowled. "Do I really have to listen to this?"

I sniffed. "Only if you've got any honor about keeping your promises." That always got to him. He slumped in a chair, and I read a story about a girl whose best friend was a bad influence on her. It couldn't have been better timing than for that story to pop up that day.

Jimmy probably didn't see how it sounded just like him, but he sure listened. That was one thing about a good story, a Christian one or not. If it was good, it kept the interest. At the end, just when you find out how everything turns out, I stopped reading out loud and made it look like I was reading to myself.

"C'mon, O'Neil! What's it say?"

"Continued tomorrow."

"You're kiddin'!"

"Yeah, I'm kidding. But there's another good story coming up tomorrow. You want to hear it?"

"Sure, the end of this one and then the next one. All right."

"No, I'll read the end of this one, but you have to come back tomorrow for the other one."

He was so eager to hear the end of the one I was reading that he agreed to everything. I didn't want to embarrass him too much when I prayed, so I kept it real short and also used the suggested prayer in the devotional book.

"Let me read the one for tomorrow."

"You mean right now?"

"No, I mean tomorrow. I'll be the reader."

I thought quick. "OK, but, you know—"

"What?"

"Well, the reader has to read everything. I mean, if you're gonna read the story, you gotta read the Bible too."

He grimaced, but he also nodded. It was time to cut the grass. He wasn't too happy about that either, but I couldn't let my friend mess up my schedule, especially on the first day.

4
Left Out

What Jimmy Calabresi and I did that morning set the schedule for the rest of the summer. Every morning, he would come by, usually before I got up, and throw rocks at my window.

I would holler something stupid down to him, he'd laugh, and I'd let him in. Sometimes he brought his own snack, other times I pretended not to notice when he swiped one of my pieces of toast or stole a quick drink of milk when he was "putting it away" for me.

It wasn't that he was hungry or anything like that. In fact, he was probably one of the richest kids in our area. That wasn't saying much. Most of the men were farmers or laborers who had a few acres. All of the mothers worked, except Mrs. Calabresi. She had twin baby boys at home and a couple of other kids between Jimmy and the twins.

So, even though his father was some kind of traveling salesman who had an office in his home, and even though they had a company car and their own car, and even though they seemed to dress nice and have the toys they wanted, there wasn't much left over for extras at their place either.

For some reason, Jimmy liked me. We had always got along together. He was the first kid I met when we moved in years ago, and while we've had our arguments, calling each other names and threatening not to invite each other to our birthday parties (which we never had anyway), we have been friends since the beginning.

When we used to bicker with each other and threaten to never see each other again, we never stayed away from each other longer than a few hours. When we saw each other the next day, we didn't apologize. We just picked up where we left off before we argued and acted as if nothing had happened.

The things we argued about never came up again. We each knew where the other one stood and what the other thought about the subject, so we avoided it. We knew each other's good points and bad points, and we sort of accepted each other.

One thing Jimmy never liked, though, was my asking him to come to church with us. I tried to tell him about my being a Christian and trying to live the way I thought God wanted me to, but he thought that was for sissies. "I never thought a sports fan, a ball player like you, would go in for that stuff, O'Neil."

If I heard him say that once, I heard it a million times. That's why he knew better when he asked about my dad's dirty magazines. He'd shown his dad's to almost every other kid in the area, and I'm not saying I wasn't curious.

In fact, I saw some pictures like that once before—a kid at school got in trouble for having them. I hated them, and yet I wanted to see them. I was curious, yet they made me sick. I just knew they were bad, and I felt guilty about wanting to see them again. I prayed a lot of times that God would forgive me for that and make the desire go away. I know He forgave me. We're still working on the desire.

About three weeks after I started staying home alone, I realized I had got used to it. I wasn't afraid. I was getting into the routine. I read my Bible and my devotional and prayed every morning whether Jimmy was there or not— and he usually was.

And, believe it or not, I got all my chores done in the morning when it wasn't so hot, and I felt so good about that

that I really enjoyed the rest of the day. Jimmy and I rode all over the place, rounding up the other guys and exploring, having bike races, playing ball, and just sitting in the sun, talking.

One morning Jimmy showed up later than usual. He didn't ask me to read him the continued story that had kept his interest for days. In fact, he didn't say much of anything. He just followed me around. That morning, my main job was weeding the garden.

Jimmy didn't like work much, especially bending over in the sun and getting dirty. But I made it look fun. I whistled, I hummed, I talked to myself. "Nothing like sprucing up the old garden, makin' room for the delicious stuff Mom planted. Can hardly wait till the weeds are gone and there's nothin' here but the dirt and the food."

Soon Jimmy was crouched right in there with me. He never got to the point of whistling or humming or talking to himself, but he got a fair amount of work done. Still, he was unusually quiet. Something was on his mind, but I had never had much luck trying to draw something out of him that he didn't want to talk about.

Finally, just before lunch, he had had enough work. "How much longer you gonna be doin' this, Dallas?"

I looked into the sky and wiped off my forehead. "It's not noon yet. Maybe twenty minutes more."

"Mind if I sit on the back porch and wait?"

"Suit yourself, Jimmy. You gotta get home for lunch?"

"Yeah, but I gotta talk to ya."

"I'm listening."

"Nah, I'll wait till you're done."

I stalled a little, just to see if he'd mosey back over and talk, but he was enjoying the shade and the breeze on the porch. When I finished weeding, I liked the feeling of the dirt caking on my hands and the sweat on my back picking up the light winds and cooling me off.

I had that good achey feeling that a hard job has been done right, and I knew Mom would be happy with it. I went to the side of the house and tugged the hose over to the back steps. Jimmy looked at me curiously while I peeled off my shirt and boots and socks.

My feet were sore and hot, and my hair was wet and matted. I grabbed a big towel that was draped over the side of the porch and tied it around my waist. Then I turned that hose on and just held it at the back of my neck.

The first several seconds worth of water were almost hot because the hose had been lying in the sun, but when the icy water from beneath the ground finally hit me, it was all I could do to keep the hose there.

Every once in a while, I'd push the nozzle up over my head and let the water splash over my hair and down my face. When I couldn't stand the cold water on my head anymore, I sprayed my feet. It was heavenly.

I closed the nozzle and dried off with the towel. Ooh, that felt good.

The whole time, Jimmy had just watched. "Wish I could do that."

"You can, Jim. What's stoppin' ya? Water's free, ya know."

"I got nothin' to change into."

"Well, you can do it at home."

"Yeah, and I gotta go."

"I thought you had something to tell me."

"I do, but it can wait."

"No, it can't. You got me curious now, so let's have it. What's going on?"

He stood and moved to the other end of the porch and looked out across the field, past the frontage road and over the highway. "You know that Park City Little League, the one that had the all-star team that made the state finals last year?"

I could hardly hear him because his back was to me, so I rolled the hose back to where I got it and wound up right under him. "Yeah, what about it?"

"They're movin' their field to right over there."

"Where?"

"Right there."

He was pointing across the highway, just on the other side. I could hardly believe it. That was the closest Little League, but we were just far enough away that we weren't allowed to join. Our parents had talked to the officials and made phone calls and even wrote letters to the editor of the local paper, but it never did any good.

My dad said he was kind of glad because it would have been hard to afford the registration, the equipment fees, and all that. I don't think he ever knew how much that hurt me. Of course, if they had allowed us, I know he would have come up with the money somewhere. He had always been a baseball fan, and he encouraged me all the time, saying I was the best young player he'd ever seen.

I should have known before I asked the next dumb question, because Jimmy wasn't sounding real happy or anything. But I asked anyway. "Does that mean they're covering a bigger area and that we can join?"

He shook his head. "No, it just means that it was costing them too much to have their fields at the junior high school, so they got some special deal and bought that land."

"Jim! That's walking distance! I mean, it can't even be half a mile! We can see it from here!"

He lowered his head and trudged back toward the steps. "All it means is that we can watch them play. Their diamonds are going to have sod and everything."

"They've got to let us play! Look how close we are."

"Forget it, Dallas. My dad already checked it out. You know what they told him? They told him we could work in the concession stands or help work on the fields. Do you believe that? We don't qualify to play in their league, but we can work for them!"

I shrugged. "I don't know. That might be kinda fun. I wonder if they'd let us umpire."

"At our age? Are you kidding?"

Of course I was kidding, but I didn't admit it yet. "Yeah, we could umpire, and when we find out the kids whose parents won't let us play, we'll make sure they're always out." I laughed loud and long, but Jimmy wasn't amused.

He moved slowly down the steps to his bike and spoke over his shoulder. "You may think it's funny, Dal, but it makes me sick. If you loved baseball as much as I do, you'd rather cry than laugh about something like this."

Just hearing him say that almost made me cry. As I stood there watching him ride off, I felt all the old feelings again. I had decided to just accept the decision the past two years and quit feeling so bad about being left out.

We had our fun. We played ball on the dead end streets. I had the best pitch, a natural sailing fastball that impressed everybody. But still, we couldn't really have a team. We weren't in any league, let alone a Little League.

And up till now, we weren't close enough to even go watch the games. I hollered to Jimmy. "I'll come over after lunch!"

"Bring your glove!"

Of course I would. I always did.

5

Bad News

The next day, I heard the heavy equipment straining at the earth on the other side of the expressway. I padded to the other end of the house and looked down on the scene from the second story hall window.

The site for the new Park City Little League diamonds was crawling with people and machines. There must have been more than a hundred parents and kids, plus several professional work crews. The parents were building wood and wire dugouts, snow fences for home run boundaries, and concession stands.

The professional men were grading the earth, trucking in sod, measuring off baselines and foul lines, and starting work on huge backstops for each diamond. The diamonds were back to back, though one had a homerun fence that looked longer all the way around.

I skipped my reading and my breakfast and dressed quickly. I sped north to Olive Street and then east to the frontage road. That was my limit to the east. I really wanted to go over the overpass and get a closer look. There was nothing more exciting than watching a perfect baseball diamond come together.

But I just rested at the far side of the frontage road, and between cars and trucks I heard the chatter of the workers and watched as a tower was erected between the two backstops.

By late morning, a gnawing hunger was working on me. I had seen a ready-made press box lifted high on the tower between the diamonds. It was great. When it was in place, hinged covers were opened so that officials and reporters could sit and watch either game.

I was just about to head for home when Jimmy arrived.

"Figured you might be here. You been here all morning?"

I nodded. "Wish I could go over, but this is my limit."

"You're kiddin'. I'm gonna go see it."

"I'll be at the house getting some lunch. Bring yours."

I expected Jimmy to show up sooner than he did. I was cleaning up the table when I heard his bike in the driveway. "Where'd you get the chips?"

Jimmy opened the bag. "Went down to Ma and Pa's on Toboggan Road. I know better than to expect anything to eat here."

"Sorry."

Jimmy waved me off as if it wasn't important and held the bag open for me. "It's worse than I thought over there."

I was surprised. "Worse than what? You mean you thought it was bad?"

"It's terrible."

"What do you mean—the ground? What?"

"How soon."

"I'm not following you."

Jimmy sighed miserably. "It's terrible how fast that place is comin' together. You know Friday night they're havin' some kinda exhibition game, and Saturday they're gonna dedicate the place?"

I shook my head. "I didn't know they could play on fresh sod that fast."

"They're not. They're only sodding the infield on the one diamond. They're going to play on dirt on the other one until the sod takes hold, then they're gonna switch and play on the sod while they plant the other. Man, even the dirt infield is smooth as glass. I was walkin' around out there."

"Pretty nice, huh?"

"Makes you wanna cry, Dal. I'm not kiddin'." Jimmy's hands and face were greasy from the chips. "Wanna throw a few? I brought my glove."

I didn't need to be coaxed. Seeing the diamond and hearing Jimmy's report just made me want to play ball. On a team. In a league. With real competition.

Jimmy crouched before the shed and smacked his free hand deep into the well of his catcher's mitt. He casually held it up as I followed through on my lazy wind up and soft first toss. The ball popped into the glove with a smack, my trademark even when I was just warming up. Jimmy talked the whole time I was getting loose.

"I saw the league president over there. You know, the tall, skinny guy with the black hair and glasses. He's got two kids on the all-star team who think they're better than they are, which is pretty good anyway. I asked him if it was true we still couldn't join the league. He got all irritated.

"Bad news. He said they had a waiting list as it was, even after they added a couple of teams before the start of the season. He also said they were starting late because of the new place and that they would have to work real hard to get all the games in. We've got to go to that game Friday night."

My arm felt good. The sun was high and hot, and I took off my shirt. I was standing the correct Little League distance from the wooden plate my father had cut from a board. "I doubt if I can go. My mother will be tired, and my sisters won't want to."

"You can go with *us*. My dad will take us."

I shook my head. "I don't think so. I don't get to see them much as it is."

Jimmy was clearly irritated, and that made me mad. I wished Jimmy felt the same way about his own family. All he seemed to care about was himself. I was loose and warm now, and I started to increase the speed on my fastball. I gripped the ball with my first and second fingers across the threads and threw with a three-quarters motion, not quite overhand.

I let my fingers tail to the right as my hand followed through, making the pitch almost a natural righthander's screw ball. The ball rocketed toward Jimmy and tailed to the right at the last instant.

Jimmy was used to it, though he hadn't expected that much speed just then. Usually I let him know when I was ready to start throwing really hard. The ball sailed to Jimmy's left and he leaped from his crouch and got the glove in front of it.

Smack!

"Yow! O'Neil, what're you doin'?" He let the ball drop and pulled off his mitt, shaking his left hand. "Tell me when you're gonna do that!" He swore. "Sorry."

"That's all right, Jimmy. My fault." I walked toward him and picked up the ball. "I just don't want you making faces when I say I would rather spend time with my sisters."

"Aah!" Jimmy never said much more than that when I was right and he was wrong. "You gonna throw some more or not? And if you are, I gotta know when you're throwing hard."

"Nah. I wanna hit some. Can you throw?"

Jimmy couldn't throw at all like I could. But what we enjoyed most was trying to hit each other's fastest pitches. Short of playing against good competition, that was as close to what we thought might make us big leaguers some day as anything else we could think of.

Since Jimmy was big and strong but for some reason didn't have the whip of an arm or the fluid motion I had, he stood almost twice as close to the shed. From that distance, I had only a fraction of a second to see the pitch, decide its speed and location, and decide whether to duck out of the way, watch it go by, or take a swing at it.

Typically, the first several of Jimmy's pitches were dangerous to any hitter. I dropped to my seat as the first one flew past my ear. I leaped like a rope jumper when the next bounced near my ankles. Then I wasn't ready when the next one buzzed right over the plate. So certain it would be another pitch that brushed me back, I was too cautious and was leaning away.

Jimmy whooped. "Strike! You took a homerun pitch! Strike!"

I smiled. "So strike me out, big shot! That's two balls and one strike."

The next pitch was fast and rising, and I swung hard. I fouled it off the end of the bat, and it sailed over the house. After another ball, Jimmy laid one right in there, and I lashed it directly back at him. Instinctively, he shot his glove up to protect his face and the ball lodged in it, knocking him on his back.

I rushed to him. "Had enough for today?"

"No way. I wanna hit."

"You sure?"

" 'Course!"

Jimmy dusted himself off and took the bat. I threw the first five pitches easily with nothing on the ball, no zip, no movement. Jimmy missed one, fouled off two, and hit the other two far and deep. I jogged after them without a word.

"Ready for some heat now?"

Jimmy crouched lower and looked more determined. I went into my usual slow windup but lifted my front leg higher. As I followed through I brought my arm down hard and fast, aiming at the outside corner of the plate.

The pitch appeared to be way outside and Jimmy relaxed. Then the ball sailed in over the inside of the plate, and he swung late, nearly falling down. I fought a smile, and Jimmy laughed. "I don't see how anybody anywhere could hit that pitch, Dal." He started to swear again and caught himself.

"I'll give you another one in the same place, Jim. It ought to be hittable if you know it's coming."

Jimmy stood back in, looking determined again. I missed my target, and the ball started out looking as if it was going right over the plate. Jimmy, confident of my control, stepped and began his swing, just as the ball rode in on him, pushing him out of the way while he swung awkwardly. The ball hit the handle end of his bat and dribbled away.

"Did you do that on purpose, O'Neil? Because if you did—"

I held up both hands. "Innocent! Innocent! No way. Sorry! I'll throw you a straight fastball, and you can blast one, all right?"

Quickly, Jimmy was back in the box. I wound up and threw directly overhand, so if there was any movement, it would be a slight rise. That's just what happened. The ball started at about waist level and rose about three inches.

Jimmy timed it perfectly, and except for the fact that he was a little under it because of the rise, he got good wood on it. The ball seemed to take off straight up but flew deep behind me. I turned to watch it.

"No wind, and that one's going over two hundred feet anyway! Nice hit, Jim!"

Jimmy beamed. "You really think so? A homer even on the Park City Little League field?"

"Absolutely. Positively. No doubt about it."

Just thinking about a ball sailing over an actual homerun fence convinced me I had to talk to my father and mother about getting permission to visit the new field. I just wanted to sit in the stands, watch a game, see the sights, smell the smells. I sort of wanted to go alone, but I knew they'd never permit that.

My dad was scheduled to call home that evening. I could never guarantee what he might allow or not allow, but at least I would be able to ask him.

I could hardly wait.

6
Drooling with Envy

My father reminded me that he did not want me going over the overpass on foot or on my bike unless I was going with someone else's father or my own mother. Dad was interested in the new Little League field and was sympathetic to my feelings about not being allowed to play.

"Are you sure you want to watch, Dal, or will that only make you feel worse?"

"I think I'd really like to, Dad. It's one thing watching the pros on television, but I kinda want to compare my pitching with other kids my own age, and I'd like to watch them hit too."

"But what if you decide you could strike 'em all out? Then you'll want to play against them."

"Yeah, but I might find out that they're too good for me too. Then I'll be glad I don't have to play against them."

Dad said that if I really wanted to go, he would talk to Mom about it. And he did. That night after the girls were in bed, Mom sat with me in the family room.

"So, your friends are going to the exhibition game to-night, huh?"

"Yeah. It's probably already over."

"I'm glad you didn't go, Dallas. Amy and Jennifer miss you terribly this summer." I nodded. I wanted to ask about the next day but didn't want to push it. "You want to go tomorrow? We could all go together."

"You really want to, Mom? Aren't you tired?"

She sighed deeply. "I sure am. But you've been doing such a good job on your chores and staying out of trouble. We can go."

"There's three games on each field, starting in the morning!"

"Oh, just pick the one you really want to see, Dallas. The girls won't sit still for three games."

"They're only six innings each!"

"One, Dallas."

I chose the second game, the one that started after lunch. I knew that four of the six returning league all-stars would be represented on the two teams, including both pitchers. When I heard the band and all the commotion at the park the next morning, though, I wished I'd chosen to watch the first game.

The sounds of the dedication wafted over the highway and past the frontage road, right onto the back porch where I sat watching my sisters play in the sand. I heard marches, the pledge to the flag, the national anthem, the Little League pledge, the introductions of the league officers, coaches, players, everything. I even heard the announcer holler, "Play ball!"

When my mother and sisters and I arrived after lunch, we had to park near the highway. The gravel parking area was jammed with cars coming in and out, dropping off players and spectators and picking up others. Mom brought snacks for the girls. For some reason, I brought my ball glove, but I felt foolish carrying it around. Before the game even started, I ran it back to the car.

My father had been right. From the beginning, I wished we hadn't come. The uniforms looked so sharp and clean and new and colorful. The field was neatly marked, and the stands were full. The players warming up looked like big leaguers.

Somehow, their uniforms made them look bigger than

their ages, even though I knew I was nearly as tall as the tallest twelve-year-olds. They practiced with a nonchalance that made them look as if they'd been playing all their lives.

It was easy for me to spot the all-stars. Jimmy Calabresi and my other friends had talked about them, so I was watching for them. By the time the game was about to begin, I was nearly sick with jealousy.

I envied the players their uniforms, their equipment, their coaches, their field, their talent, their teams, their league, their umpires, everything. The feeling started in the pit of my stomach. I wasn't hungry. I was hurting.

As the game began, the crowd grew quiet. The first pitch was a strike, nice and slow, right down the middle, as if the pitcher had aimed. I knew that if Jimmy Calabresi had been at bat and suspected a cream puff pitch like that, he'd have deposited it in the parking lot out beyond the center field fence.

Soon I realized that the pitcher had simply been eager to get a strike on the hitter. None of his next offerings were anything like the first. He came back with a slow curve that dropped and fooled the hitter, making him swing and miss.

Ahead no balls and two strikes, he wasted a fastball that went into the dirt on the outside of the plate. The catcher made a circus catch, but I hardly noticed. I was still reeling from the speed of the pitch.

The next one was even faster. It hit in front of the plate and bounced high on the backstop. My eyes followed the catcher as he jogged back for it, but for some reason everyone was screaming and pointing to first base where all the action was.

The batter had taken off running and was easily safe. But half the crowd had missed the fact that the batter had swung at the third strike, even though it had bounced in front of him and over his head. Since the catcher missed the ball, the hitter was free to advance to first.

Now the pitcher was mad, but instead of coming unraveled he settled down and struck out the next two hitters on six straight fastballs. I was amazed. Each pitch seemed to hit the same spot, on the inside corner where it looked big and hittable but was coming in too fast for them to get the bat around in time.

If they took the pitch, it was a strike. If they swung, they missed. The problem was, the number four hitter on the visiting team was a fastball hitter, a power hitter. But the pitcher knew that. They had been teammates on the all-star team that finished fourth in the state, and all of a sudden it was if the pitcher didn't have a fastball at all.

He threw every pitch on the outside part of the plate, low and curving away from the big hitter. He missed the first two, then drove the third on a line up the middle, right to the glove of the centerfielder who didn't have to move even a step.

I was so intent on studying the pitchers and the hitters and the level of play that I hardly noticed that my mother had lost interest in the game and was wandering around behind the stands, keeping an eye on my little sisters.

If the game hadn't been close and exciting, I would have wanted to leave early. I knew my mother and sisters were only there because Mom felt she owed me some fun. It wasn't interesting for them, and it was making me sick.

Then my friends showed up, Jimmy Calabresi leading the way. "We've been watching the other game, Dallas. We missed you last night. Where were you?"

"Didn't come." I greeted all the guys. Brent, Cory, Loren, Ryan, Bugsy, Toby, and Derek. They were basically up to no good. Hollering at the players, being obnoxious, loud, and rude. In truth, they were all drooling with envy. I could hardly blame them. They all lived in the square mile around my house. All loved baseball. All were ineligible to play in the Park City Little League.

Bugsy, black and wiry, had quit watching the game. He was pinching and poking and laughing. "Call us the rejects! Lepers! Unclean!"

I was embarrassed. "C'mon, Bugs. Knock it off." People

were staring, wondering who this scruffy bunch was and why we were causing such a scene.

Jimmy joined right in. "Yeah! The Frontage Road Flunkies! That's us!"

Brent, a quiet blond with big eyes and a tiny body, stepped down to sit next to me. "You could hit this guy."

I shook my head. I'd been watching the visiting pitcher. He had excellent control, had walked only one batter, and kept the ball low. He seemed calm and self-assured on the mound. Very professional. And fast. There was no way, at least without a lot of practice, that I could come near this guy.

Brent still looked at me. "None of these guys could hit you."

That warmed me up some. "Some of 'em could. Others I could get out. Others *you* could get out."

"Me? I'm an infielder. I don't even wanna pitch."

I smiled, still keeping my eyes on the game. "I'm trying to say more about their weak hitting than your pitching, Brent."

The rest of the guys always seemed to follow my lead, and when they gradually realized that I was not in a mood to be rowdy—they probably thought it was because my mother was there, but it wasn't—and that I was carefully studying the game, they did the same. Soon we all sat, hunched forward, staring at the field, intent on every play.

In the top of the fifth inning, the visiting team blew the game wide open when the opposing pitcher lost his control and his cool and began walking hitters and arguing with his coach, his teammates, and the umpires. He made an embarrassing scene.

That was all I could take. The game was no longer interesting. The pitcher, who had wonderful talent, had wasted it by losing his temper. And I was irritated that he was allowed to get away with it. More important, I was hurt that the pitcher would abuse the privilege of playing on a diamond like this, with all the extras that went with it.

I had to leave. I scrambled down to behind the stands where I found my mother and sisters. "We can go."

Mom was concerned. "Are you sure, Dallas? Your friends are here. And we don't mind. The girls are having fun."

"They'll have more fun at home. And the guys and I might have more fun playing ball on our own side of the highway anyway."

7

The Baker Street Sports Club

It was that afternoon, as the guys from the other side of the highway (as I called them) sat around in an open field on Toboggan Road, that the idea for the Baker Street Sports Club was born.

Nine boys, nine ball gloves, and eight bikes (Ryan had ridden on Toby's handlebars) were parked well off the road. No one spoke for a long time. Our minds were on what we had seen at the new Park City Little League field.

I felt a little guilty. The guys had always looked up to me. They had all tried to hit that crazy sailing pitch of mine, and only Bugsy and Brent had ever come close to beating me in a race. Loren and I were the oldest of the bunch, but Loren was quiet. While a good outfielder, he wasn't a fast runner.

Yet not even I had much to say on this depressing day. I knew our problem was that we were all jealous of the Little Leaguers, and we all felt left out, rejected, second class. For about ten minutes we just sat in the dirt, tracing circles with our fingers.

That reminded me of my dad and made me feel even worse. The boys spoke infrequently between batting away the pesky flies. The conversation didn't mean much. Just idle talk.

It was Brent, a slim whippet of a young boy who could chase down any fly ball within a block of him, who finally said what was on everyone's mind. "They don't want us in their league because they think we're not good enough for 'em."

Ryan spoke up. "I'll bet they all have bikes. I'd get laughed right outa the place."

Jimmy shook his head. "Just because they have lots of money, how come they're scared of us? They've never seen country people before? It's not like we're all farmers."

I grunted. "None of us are, but all of us wish we were. I'm not ashamed of it."

Not to be outdone, Jimmy stayed in the conversation. "Neither am I! In fact, I wish my dad *was* a farmer."

Somebody laughed. "Your dad's hands haven't ever even been dirty, Calabresi."

"They were too! I remember once last year!" And that made everybody laugh even more. I liked it better like this, when we were excited about something, having fun.

But we fell silent again, and someone remembered what was said at the ballgame. "We're the Frontage Road Flunkies."

I had heard enough. I stood and straddled my bike. The rest looked at me as if wondering if I was about to leave. I wasn't. "We're not either flunkies. We shouldn't even kid about that. We're not rejects. We're not lepers. We're ball players. We've been playing together how long now?"

Bugsy looked up, as if in thought. "More'n five years."

I nodded. "That's a long time. I wouldn't even want to be in that league if they'd break us up, and you know they would. One on this team, two on that, a couple more on another. That wouldn't be good. It wouldn't be right. It wouldn't be fun."

"We're our own team."

"Yeah."

"Yeah. The Frontage Road Fl—"

I interrupted. "Don't say it. There's got to be a better name."

"Right, Dallas. Come up with a good name for our baseball team."

I was thinking. "We're not just a baseball team, though. We're a football team too. And a soccer team. We're anything we want to be. We're a sports club."

"The Frontage Road Sports Club?"

"Will you get off that Frontage Road kick?"

"The Olive Street Oilers, get it? Olive Oil?"

"Nah."

"The Toboggan Road Tigers?"

"Maybe. We're ferocious."

"Ah, who would we play even if we did have a team?"

"Forget that till we come up with a name. We gotta have a name. How many live on Baker Street?"

Toby, Ryan, Jimmy, and Cory raised their hands. I spoke softly, as if only to myself, looking into the distance. "The Baker Street Sports Club."

It was right. It was perfect. It sounded so good no one said anything for a while. Soon they were all talking at once.

"We're more than a team. We're a club."

"We could have meetings. A club house."

"A president."

"A treasurer."

"For what? We got no money."

"Who'd be president?"

"We'd have to vote."

"No, it would have to be Dallas."

"No, we'd have to vote."

"OK, let's vote."

I wanted to think about it some more. "Let's play ball and talk about it later."

"We need a bat."

I looked at Jimmy.

Jimmy smiled. "Be right back." He rode off for his bat.

Without any discussion, I started sending different boys to different positions on our imaginary field. The weeds were deep. There were tree stumps and fallen trunks around. The ground was uneven. A ground ball would go

51

nowhere. And anyone brave enough to keep his eye on a fly ball would find himself on his face in a second or two.

"We want to try to hit your pitching!"

"Yeah, let's play at your place!"

I held up my hand. "Monday, after lunch."

"Why not tomorrow?"

"I'm busy all day."

They knew why. I'd invited most of them to church more than once. "Are we gonna organize our club on Monday?"

"You betcha."

"We gonna have rules?"

"Of course. But we have to elect a president first."

"Let's call it a captain instead."

"Whatever."

"It's going to be you, Dallas."

"We can't be sure of that yet." I wasn't just trying to be modest. I thought maybe Jimmy would want to be in charge. Or Bugsy.

"Yes, we can." It was Brent. Soft-spoken Brent. He had said it with such force and authority that everyone stopped talking. He was staring right at me. "We can be sure. Dallas is the only logical choice."

Cory was nodding his red head. I was afraid to look at Jimmy. Loren shrugged. "I have no problem with that. He'll be fair. As long as he doesn't make us all start prayin' or somethin'." Everyone laughed.

Ryan and Toby looked at each other. "What do you think, Ry?" Toby nodded.

Bugsy held out a hand to me, and I shook it without enthusiasm. "I'll make it unanimous, Dal."

"That doesn't make it unanimous." It was Derek. "There's still Jimmy and me."

I was afraid of that. It wasn't that I wanted or needed to be in charge, but I was willing if everyone wanted me. If even one person didn't want me, I didn't want to do it.

Derek spoke again. "I'll vote for Dallas. No question."

Finally, I had to look at Jimmy. And for the first time since I'd met the big catcher, I couldn't read him. I had no idea what he was thinking. Jimmy wasn't looking at me. He was looking at each of his friends one at a time. They all met his gaze, staring straight back at him.

Finally, he spoke. "Nobody forced this. It wasn't a set up. If I was doing the choosing all by myself, I wouldn't have done it any differently. But, Dallas, if you're our president or captain or whatever, what are we going to do? Just be a fun club, or what?"

I shrugged. "I don't know. Whatever you guys want, I guess."

Jimmy shook his head. "No, that's not good enough. We got to have a reason. We got to do something."

I knew what he was driving at. "Well, sure, first thing is we need to start a team, be a team. We already are a team."

"You mean with positions and a batting order and all that?"

"Well, yeah, sure. That sounds good."

"What else?"

"Well, give me time to think about it."

Jimmy was pushing. "Think about it now, Dallas. Who will we play? Anybody?"

"You mean will we challenge the Park City Little League?"

Jimmy turned to the rest of the guys with a startled look. "No, that's not what I meant at all, Dallas. But what a great idea! I think we made the right choice, boys. What do you think?"

They responded by crowding around me and clapping me on the back.

8

Rodney Blasingame

I did a lot of thinking over the weekend, and by Monday afternoon I had a list of things to talk over with the club members. "We are the Baker Street Sports Club. Each of us is a charter member if we agree to the rules and join today. We don't have cards or patches or uniforms or anything like that, but we're a club anyway.

"Here are the rules. We will practice our sports every chance we get. We'll teach each other and learn from each other. We won't fight and argue. We'll be good sports. We'll look for a place to play our games, and we'll try to get some competition. Right now I don't know how or where. If there is anyone we know who can help coach us, we'll ask them. Otherwise, we'll do it all on our own. If somebody checks out a book from the library on how to play a sport better, he'll tell us about it or pass it around.

"And no, nobody has to pray or anything unless they want to. But I read a story and some verses from the Bible every morning. Jimmy's been listening, and if anybody else wants to come and listen, I'll move it out to my front porch. But nobody has to come unless he wants to."

We played ball all afternoon, with me hitting ground balls and then fly balls and then pitching to everybody for several minutes each. The guys seemed excited, thrilled that they had made their friendship and their common interest official.

I had one last instruction for them before they headed home for dinner. "Same time, same place tomorrow." Our land wasn't the best for practicing on, but it was the best we had. It was not nearly big enough for a regulation diamond, but at least it was smooth in spots. That was something else we had to work on.

I expected to see them all the next afternoon. I didn't know what to expect the next morning.

That evening when my mother got home, I could tell she was terribly upset. She was quieter than usual, a little crabbier, especially with the girls, and generally seemed she had something on her mind.

My dad always had ways of getting her to talk, but he wasn't scheduled to call until the next evening, and when she noticed that on the calendar, she seemed to sag. I put my arm around her, which was something I hadn't done since I was much younger.

"Need someone to talk to, Mom?"

"Do I! Let me get the girls to bed first."

I was kind of shocked. I knew something was on her mind, but I didn't think she'd really talk to me about it. We lounged in the family room with cups of hot chocolate, and she told me a story.

"You know that the Blasingames, the family I'm babysitting for, also have a son who graduated from high school this month, don't you?"

"I guess so. I hadn't really thought about it."

"He's a good boy, Dallas. I think. He's not going to be eighteen even until this fall, and his parents think he's too young for college, though they would like him to go to Harvard or Yale. He didn't get good enough grades for that, but they have so much money, they think they might be able to get him in anyway."

She sighed and looked out the window. "I had wondered why they didn't have *him* babysit this summer, since he's not working and isn't planning on going to school in the fall, but now I can see why."

It wasn't like my mother to take so long getting to the point. "Why, Mom?"

"Well, he's so immature, so irresponsible. You know, Dallas, you have more wisdom and responsibility than Rodney, and he's nearly six years older than you are."

That made me feel good, but I was still curious about this guy. "What's his problem?"

"Well, the only thing he did in high school was charm the teachers and coaches to death, so he graduated without too much problem. He was always in trouble for breaking rules. Nothing bad, just lots of mischief. He was interested only in sports."

I smiled. "He can't be all bad."

"Well, I know you're a sports guy, Dallas, but you have other interests too, and you keep them all in perspective."

I wasn't too sure, but I nodded anyway. I wanted her to keep talking.

"This is a good looking boy, Dallas, with lots of potential. I don't see too much of him because he's sleeping when I get there, and he usually just heads out to run around with his friends and play ball all afternoon. But this morning he wanted to talk."

"About what?"

"About something he did last night. He and his friends are in a baseball league that plays night games in the City League. I guess he's the only rich kid on any of the teams, and so he takes a lot of teasing. They call him Pretty Boy and Money Bags and stuff like that. That only makes him play harder, and he's earned their respect by being one of the better young players in the league."

"Why do they call him Pretty Boy?"

"Well, he's real pale and has very dark, curly hair. Quite a good looking boy. Girls call for him all the time. But he's hardly ever home. I think answering the phone is one of the biggest jobs I have in that house."

"So, what did he want to talk about this morning?"

Mom folded her arms and looked down. "He was feeling

guilty about something he did last night, and he wanted to tell someone. The strange thing was, it was something he did alone, after he and his friends had gone out drinking and cruising around and pulling pranks."

"What kinds of pranks?"

"Oh, funny stuff. Things your father and I would never want to think you were doing, but mostly harmless yelling and screeching tires and maybe tossing firecrackers up on someone's porch."

"That's harmless?"

"Well, not the firecrackers, of course. No. In fact it's all very immature, but not worth his needing someone to confess it to."

I was beginning to wonder if she was ever going to tell me what the serious prank was.

"He asked me when I would have time to talk to him, and I told him in the afternoon when the little ones were down for naps. Rather than sleeping till noon or eating all morning, he just hung around the house, watching some television and not saying anything. Normally he's very polite but always in a hurry to get out of the house.

"Finally, we talked. He said I seemed like a person he could trust, someone he could talk to without worrying that whatever he told me would get back to his parents. I told him that I would keep a secret if he had something to tell me. And he did."

"What was it?"

"Well, I had never heard of this, Dallas. Maybe you have. He says he cut a cookie or did a cookie cutter or something like that on someone's lawn. Have you ever heard of anything like that?"

"Sure. That's when you drive right up on their lawn and turn real sharp and step on the gas. You slide all over the place and head back for the street, and if the ground is soft enough, you tear up the lawn something awful."

It was if a light went on in Mom's head. "Oh, OK, all right, that explains it. He said he didn't even know why he did it, because he was alone and wasn't showing off to his

58

buddies or anything. He was still a little high from drinking, but he doesn't take drugs, and he wasn't drunk, at least in his opinion. Anyway, he said he had been driving around, not tired enough to go home to bed, and he found himself in a modest, residential section with neat lawns and little flower beds. And he just got the urge to do a cookie cutter on one of the lawns.

"There were no lights on in any of the houses as far as he could see, but one beautiful home at a corner had a flood light illuminating the front lawn. He said it was big and perfect and inviting, so he just gunned the engine."

"What kind of car does he drive, Mom?"

"Oh, I don't know. Some kind of foreign, small, black thing with a name that's just initials."

"BMW?"

"Yes, that could be it. Why?"

"Just wonderin'."

"So he drove up over the curb, just missed a fire hydrant, spun around twice in the yard, and raced off. He said by the time he hit the street again, two lights came on in the house, and he thought he saw someone opening the front door.

"That scared him, but he knew no one could have gotten out the door in time to see his car, so he decided to double back in a few minutes. He drove around a while and then went back into that neighborhood to survey the damage he'd done. He said that up to that point it was fun, and he was excited about having pulled it off."

I was puzzled. "But now he feels guilty about it?"

"He has a reason to, Dallas. When he got back, there was an ambulance in the driveway of that same house, red lights flashing. Neighbors were out from all over the block. Paramedics were hunched over an old man lying on his back on the porch. He was in pajamas and robe, and his wife was crying.

"Rodney risked someone recognizing his car and parked at the side of the street and stood with the neighbors on the sidewalk. They were all complaining about the vandals who had done this and how Mr. Slater might die, with his bad heart and all. Rodney slipped away and drove home. Said he didn't sleep much last night and has been listening to the news to see how the old gentleman is."

I was stunned by the story. And one thing left me curious. Why was my mother convinced that Rodney Blasingame was such a good kid at heart?

9

Jimmy's Problem

Mom felt the need to explain what she meant even before I had the chance to ask. "I know everyone is born in sin and that none of us is truly good at heart. But Rodney is not the typical rebellious young person. There's something soft, something tender inside. He's scared. He feels bad. He's worried."

"But it doesn't sound like he felt that way until he found out someone might have been hurt by what he did."

"That's just the point, Dallas. And that's different from feeling bad only because you got caught. He didn't mean to hurt anyone. Now that he has, or might have, he realizes that even damaging an old couple's property could be an expensive burden for them. It woke him up, Dallas, and that tells me he's a different kind of a kid."

I shrugged. I didn't know. I hadn't ever met him. "What's he going to do?"

"I don't know. I told him to confess."

"I'll bet he laughed in your face."

"No, he didn't. It made sense to him. I didn't want to come on too strong, but I quoted Scripture for him too, about sin and confession and repentance. Sometimes, Dallas, people listen to you only when they're at their lowest point."

"Did he get mad?"

"Not really. He got a little quiet. He didn't talk about God or what I'd quoted to him, but he was going to spend the rest of the day finding out the full name of the couple, seeing if the man was all right, and offering to pay for the damages."

"He has money?"

"A sea of money, Dallas. He has trust funds that become available to him when he turns eighteen, twenty-one, and twenty-five."

"But what about now, before he's eighteen?"

"He has plenty of money now too."

"So, what did he find out?"

"That's just it. He wasn't back by the time I left. He had another game tonight, but he would have had to have been back early to change into his uniform if he was going to make it in time. A couple of his buddies on the team called looking for a ride to the game."

"So you think he found the people?"

"I guess. But I'm worried. I mean, there's nothing to worry about, I guess, unless they don't forgive him and want to get back at him somehow."

Mom went to bed looking just as upset as she had when she got home, but there was no way for her to check without calling the Blasingames, and she had promised Rodney she would not tell his parents. He promised to do that when the time was right.

The next morning, every charter member of the Baker Street Sports Club except Jimmy Calabresi showed up on my front porch. I read the devotional, read the Bible, and prayed. No one said anything or asked anything or made any jokes. They looked a little embarrassed, but as soon as I was finished, they asked how many episodes there were to the story. I told them there were plenty to keep us going all summer. They cheered and headed for the shed.

When I had thrown batting practice for an hour or so, someone suggested we get our own clubhouse. I shrugged. "Where would we find one?"

"How about your shed, Dal?"

"Nah. It's full. Anyway it stinks, and it's too hot. My dad would never allow it. We need a place near a field we can turn into a ball field."

Everybody looked at each other. "Man, Dallas, you come up with the greatest ideas. But where would we find that?"

I didn't know, but I'd been thinking about it. "Maybe I'll talk to Mrs. Ferguson."

"Mrs. Ferguson? I'm afraid of her."

"Why?"

"I thought she was mean."

I smiled. "You must've done something bad to her, because she's wonderful. I'll go talk to her about that acreage down by her stream off Baker Street."

"Should anybody go with you, Dallas?"

"I was thinkin' about taking Jimmy, but I don't know where he is this morning."

"Here he comes!"

Jimmy was pedalling toward us from way down the road. "I'll go talk to him, and we'll visit Mrs. Ferguson. You guys can't stay here when I'm not here, so let's meet back here after lunch."

I jumped on my bike and raced out to meet Jimmy. "Where were you? I didn't expect to see everyone else, but I did expect you to be there."

Jimmy looked down. "I dunno."

"You do too. Now what's wrong?"

"Well, Dallas, I liked hearing the stories every morning, and I didn't even mind the other parts, you know, the Bible and all that. But when it's everybody, well—"

"You mean you just wanted it to be you and me?"

Jimmy nodded but wouldn't look at me.

"I didn't know that, Jim."

"Well, you should have."

"How could I?"

"We're best friends!"

"That doesn't mean I can read your mind."

"Well, you should know."

"You want to read today's story, just the two of us?"

65

Now Jimmy was angry and embarrassed. "No!"

"Well, what *do* you want?"

"I don't know. I'm just in a bad mood."

I told him my plan to visit Mrs. Ferguson. He was sure I didn't really want him to go.

"You're just inviting me to get me out of my bad mood."

"I am not, but if you don't get out of it, I'm gonna belt you out of it. Were you really late today because all the other guys were there?"

He looked down and nodded.

I didn't believe him. "The truth, Jim."

"I'm a little jealous, I guess."

"Of what?"

"Of you. I wouldn't mind bein' everybody's favorite."

"Jim! Everybody likes you!"

"Not like they like you."

"That's not all it's cracked up to be. You think I like always being the one who has to decide everything? Nobody wants to do anything unless I want to. It's too much responsibility, really, and there are lots of times when I'd just like to be one of the guys and do what somebody else wants to do."

"Why don't you then and let me be captain?"

"That'd be fine with me! You want me to suggest it?"

"No! Let me suggest it."

"But they might do it if I suggest it, Jimmy."

"And they won't if I suggest it, huh?"

"Well, they voted me in, so they have to listen to me."

"Forget it. You're just trying to make me look bad. If I suggest it, everybody thinks I'm only looking out for myself. And if you suggest it, they think you're just trying to be nice to me."

"What if I said I had changed my mind and was resigning, and I was picking you to replace me?"

Jimmy looked up at me. "You'd do that?"

"If our friendship depended on it. If it's what you want. I was flattered that the other guys wanted me to be captain of the club, but it's no big deal to me. I'd just as soon let you do it and just be part of the team. Hey, where's your glove and bat?"

"I didn't bring 'em."

"You were on your way to my house. You would've needed 'em."

"I wasn't really. I was just gonna ride by there and see who showed up. Everybody but me, huh?"

I nodded.

"Actually I was headed to the Little League park to look around again. Wanna come?"

"No, Jimmy. I'm worried about you. Even you voted for me. You were the last one. You said you couldn't have made the decision better yourself."

"What was I supposed to say when it was unanimous up till then?"

"So you weren't serious?"

"Of course I was serious. I just didn't know it was going to make me jealous."

"It's not that important to me, Jim. I mean that. If you really want me to, I'll quit and tell them you'll be taking over."

Jimmy didn't say anything for a long time. Then he nodded. "That's what I want."

I didn't know how the other guys would take it. Actually, I was surprised. I thought Jimmy would change his mind when I put it that way. But he didn't. And so we rode off to Mrs. Ferguson's with Jimmy as next captain of the Baker Street Sport Club.

Mrs. Ferguson is a tall, bony old woman who looks a little frightful but is actually a warm, wonderful woman. Her husband had died before any us us were born, but she still talks of him often.

Jimmy introduced himself as captain of our club and said we had something to ask her. She was impressed. "My, isn't that an important position?" But she kept looking at me. "You boys want any cookies? Baked some yesterday."

I started to shake my head, but Jimmy said he'd love

some. She brought in a big plateful, and, while munching, Jimmy told her our idea and popped the question.

"Our sports club has a baseball team, and we need some of your property for a ball field. Is it OK?"

I cringed. What a way to talk to somebody, let alone an old widow lady! She was too crafty for Jimmy anyway.

"Is what OK?"

"If we use some of your property to play ball on."

She scowled. "Well, not near the house, of course."

Jimmy shook his head, as if disgusted with her. "Of course not. I'm talkin' about all the useless land down there in front of your creek. We'd just have to smooth it out some. And you've got that shed down there that we could use for a meeting place. There's only nine of us now, but there might be more later. How about it?"

Luckily, Jimmy had spoken so quickly, Mrs. Ferguson had missed most of the insult of the way he had asked. I had to speak up. I began slowly. "Mrs. Ferguson, I have something to ask you." She looked at me sweetly, as if relieved that she could talk to someone she recognized and who would speak slowly and courteously.

"You've lived around here longer than any of us, and my parents and my little sisters and I have enjoyed your cooking and gifts from your garden for years. What I was wondering was whether you'd be willing to let us do some work on your property. Like Jimmy said, we have a sports club, and we need some open land where we can put in bases and maybe a small backstop and be able to practice and play.

"We'd take good care of it, and we'd be happy to do other work for you in exchange for the privilege of using it. If that old shed was not needed for anything else, we could fix that up for you too. And before winter, we'd leave everything just the way we found it."

She stood without a word and motioned us with a finger to follow her through the house to the kitchen in the back. She looked down on the piece of land we were talking about from the window over her kitchen sink.

She looked warily at Jimmy, then more softly at me. "And you'd take personal responsibility, Dallas?"

I glanced at Jimmy. "I'd be happy to, ma'am, if that's what you'd like."

"That's what I'd like. And I wouldn't want you boys running around the other parts of the property or playing near the house or making a lot of noise where I could hear you."

I nodded. "And we wouldn't do any work on the land without telling you first."

"What kind of work did you have in mind?"

"Well, you can see that the land is overrun with weeds and big rocks. And there are some branches and fallen trees. We'd have to clear all of that."

"How would you do it?"

"Teamwork and my dad's tractor—the small one. The place will look really nice when it's done."

She looked at us both and then gazed out the window again. She spoke softly, and we could hardly hear her. "Carl was an athlete, you know. Well, of course, you wouldn't know. He's been gone longer than you've been alive. But he loved baseball. Was crazy about it, if the truth be known. Would have loved to have had his own field right here, I'm sure, if he'd had the time."

Turning back to me, she had a twinkle in her eye. She pointed at me. "You're the key person here, Dallas O'Neil. You're the one I'll deal with, and you'll answer to me, hear?"

I nodded.

"And under one more condition, I'll let you and the rest of the boys in your club start using the land right now."

"What condition?"

"You finish that plate of cookies."

10
Baker Street Field

I was full from breakfast, but just as Jimmy was helping himself to a half dozen more cookies, I asked Mrs. Ferguson if I could take them back to the rest of the club and we'd promise to eat every last one.

She transferred them to a paper bag, and on our way out the door, Jimmy turned back. *What now?* I wondered.

"I have something I need to say to you, Mrs. Ferguson. I was just kidding about me being captain of the Baker Street Sports Club. Dallas is captain. Always was. Always will be."

She looked confused but perfectly happy to have been informed. "Very well, boys. Have fun."

We pedalled back to my place as fast as we could, but no one had returned yet. We were so excited we nearly finished off the cookies, and I skipped lunch. We sat on the back porch, making plans about how we'd fix up the land to make a useable baseball field.

When we ran out of things to say, we sat in silence for a while before Jimmy finally spoke again. "Dallas, you won't tell anybody what I said about wanting to be captain, will you?"

"Nah. Don't worry about it."

"'Cause I was just kiddin', ya know."

"No, I don't know that, Jimmy. I won't say anything, but don't try to say you weren't serious, because you were."

He frowned and nodded. Maybe I shouldn't have been so easy on him, but what are friends for?

When the guys started showing up again, Jimmy and I held onto the news until they were all there. When I announced the location of our new field, everybody jumped and cheered. We planned work details and made equipment assignments, and within an hour we were all working feverishly on the weedy field on the Ferguson spread.

Finally, we were ready for me to bring down my dad's lawn tractor to cut the tall weeds and to attach a chain and pull rocks and trees out of the way. I phoned my mother to see if it was all right. The only thing she was worried about was safety and money. "And Dallas, I'm going to count on you for both. You must tell all the other boys where to stand and what to watch out for, and only you can drive the tractor. As for the gas, that will have to come out of your money. And if anything happens to the tractor, well, you know."

"I know. Thanks, Mom."

"Also, Dallas, I have the best news imaginable about Rodney Blasingame. I'll tell you all about it when I get home." She did, but I saved the news and didn't tell any of the other guys for almost a month.

The field wasn't even ready for practicing on for more than a week. We bought several dollars worth of gasoline and oil, and I even snapped two chains. We raised money by cutting other peoples' lawns and doing odd jobs around the neighborhood. The Baker Street Sports Club was getting a reputation. A good one.

Our field was smooth but had interesting rises here and there. It wasn't perfect the way the Park City Little League field was perfect. In fact, we learned to catch crazily bouncing grounders and to snag flies while churning up and down little inclines.

The best part was that Ryan's father donated the fence sections from an old dog kennel he replaced, and we attached them to stakes we drove into the ground with a sledge hammer from Toby's garage. That gave us a small but very useful backstop.

We looked for cheap snow fencing for a home run wall, but we weren't even close to having enough for the five fifty-foot sections we'd need. We raised enough money for a half dozen new balls, two aluminum bats—which we didn't like but we knew were necessary because they wouldn't break—and then we made our biggest purchase. It took all our leftover cash, and I even had to borrow from my untouchable fund that I kept under my bed. All nine of us went to the sporting goods store and picked out three bases, a home plate, and a pitching rubber.

We bought a score book that had the Little League dimensions in it, and we carefully measured the foul lines and chalked them. Now we had everything. Everything except real competition. We practiced from the middle of the morning until supper time every night, and after supper we practiced until dark.

We took turns playing with three guys hitting and six in the field, and one of the hitters was the catcher. There were no walks, and the pitcher could throw as hard as he wanted. We ran, we hit, we slid, we threw. We were in heaven.

Some of the other boys' fathers started showing up to watch, and they got excited. A couple of them gave us some pointers on how to play better, and a few others bought us batting helmets and some catcher's equipment. We had speed and good arms, and at least five of us were decent hitters.

We were clean and fast in the infield, and it seemed we were planning for a big game. Only we knew there wouldn't be one. We begged Mr. Calabresi to talk the Little League president into letting us play against one of their teams, even if a Park City team came to our field. They'd probably laugh at us, but we'd have the home field advantage.

We offered to play against some of their teams just for practice on their non-game days. We tried to challenge local softball teams. Nobody would do it. There were problems of insurance and regulations and all that.

Every once in a while we talked some kids from another area into coming over to see our field and playing a few innings. Even some of the kids from the Little League showed up now and then. But we never played our nine guys against another team. We had no idea how good we were. We just thought we were great.

The field took away some of the appeal of my morning devotions with the team, but when fewer of them came every morning, I just took my story book to the field, and they listened there.

Mr. Calabresi came back with the bad news. "No way. They can't let you play on their field, and they won't allow their teams to play here."

I was as disappointed as anyone. It wasn't fair. "What if one of their teams wants to come over here on their own?"

He shook his head. "I guess they couldn't stop them, but their coaches couldn't come. Or their umpires. And they couldn't wear their uniforms."

I had an idea. "I don't care. We're going to challenge their best team. I'll even write a letter to the editor of the newspaper. That'll get people to know about us and our field. At least we'll get people out here to see us. If the Little League won't allow it, maybe their players will have some pride and show us if they've got guts."

If they did, I'd tell my team the good news about Rodney Blasingame. Because it would affect every one of us.

While waiting for my letter to the editor to be published, I secretly went to the mothers of each of the members of the Baker Street Sports Club and got the boys' clothing sizes. I reported them back to my mother who gave them to Rodney Blasingame. I was almost ready to tell my teammates what was going on.

Finally, my letter to the editor was published. In it, I told the whole story of our area and my friends. I also wrote about our attempts to play in the Park City Little League (especially now that they were so close) and of our building our own ball park. Then I simply asked for some competition.

Not long after my letter to the editor was published, another letter ran from John Stephenson, the father of one of the Park City Little League all-stars. He wrote that he was no coach and that, while it wouldn't be approved by the league, he would see that enough players from his son's team would come to our new field to accept our challenge.

Mr. Stephenson promised to pay for two umpires, if I, the writer of the original letter, would just call to confirm everything and settle on a date. He was very nice when I called and suggested that the game be an old fashioned sandlot style where you play until dark, win, lose, or tie, and neither team uses a coach.

His son Gary's team had a Saturday morning game in two weeks, so they would be available that afternoon. "Remember, their coaches can't be involved, and it's not associated with the Little League. This is just a bunch of kids getting together for a ball game."

"OK! Yes, sir!" I was so excited I couldn't stand it. I told my mother I was going to tell the good news to the Baker Street Sports Club the next day.

"All the good news, Dallas?"

"Yes. All of it."

"Let me make a phone call first."

When she came back, she had a huge smile. "Rodney would like to tell your team his news himself."

"You're kidding."

"No, he'll meet you here tomorrow, and you can have all the guys in for lunch. I'll have everything ready."

"I can have everybody in here by myself?"

"Rodney will be here. I've come to trust him."

I called all the guys and told them to come for lunch. At first they thought I was kidding. The next day they found out I wasn't. They started showing up around eleven in the morning, and when they were all there, I read the story, read from the Bible, and prayed.

Nobody complained, but it was kind of hard to keep them all quiet when they knew something was up, and just before lunch I told them that a guest was coming. It was good timing. Rodney pulled in the driveway just then, and the guys ran to the windows. "Who is it? Who's that?"

"You'll find out."

Rodney introduced himself to me, and I introduced him to everyone else as the son of the family my mother was babysitting for. "The Blasingames of Blasingame's Fashions." Lunch was strange and awkward because everyone was wondering why he was there.

Rodney mostly talked baseball with the kids near him. Then it was time for the news. "What have you told them so far, Dallas?"

"Nothing. I guess my news comes first."

He nodded.

I told the guys about my conversation with Mr. Stephenson and that the game was set for Saturday. I had a hard time quieting them down. Then it was Rodney's turn. He had been friendly and outgoing at the table, but now he seemed very nervous, almost as if he was about to cry.

"I'm here because I was assigned by a judge to be here." He told them the story of his cutting a cookie on the Slater's lawn and how my mother talked to him about God's forgiveness. "She encouraged me to find the Slaters and make things right.

"By the time I found them, the police were already looking for whoever it was who had done that and had caused Mr. Slater to have a heart attack. Fortunately, he's doing fine now. The strange thing was, they decided to drop the charges."

"What's that mean?"

"They didn't want me to get in trouble because I said I was sorry and offered to pay for the damages. Seems they were Christians too, just like the O'Neils. But the judge in the case said he wanted something even better to come of all this. While he appreciated my coming forward to admit what I had done, he said I should not be let off too lightly.

"He assigned me to not only pay for the damage to their yard, but to also help repair it. Which I've done. And he assigned me to not only pay for any of Mr. Slater's medical bill not covered by insurance, but to also help in his therapy. Which I have also done.

"And then he told me to find a worthy cause to donate some more time and money to. When Mrs. O'Neil told me about your club and your problems, I asked the judge if that was worthy enough. And that's why I'll be coaching you guys for the next week—except during the game when no coaches are allowed.

"That's also why I made a major purchase for you at my father's Chicago garment factory. For the past several weeks, one of their top projects has been to sew uniforms for the Baker Street Sports Club baseball team. I have them in the car."

I expected all the whooping and hollering we'd grown used to, but the guys were stunned. They were silent. A few of us went out to help Rodney cart in the boxes, and suddenly my living room was full of kids in their underwear, trying on brand new baseball uniforms, socks, shoes, hats, and all.

They were gorgeous. The shoes and socks and undershirts were blue. The uniforms were gray with red, white, and blue pinstriping, and each had a number on the front and back. I was number four. The shirts were V-necked with the same piping, and on the chest and the hat was the letter *B*.

The guys were almost in tears, they looked and felt so good. Every uniform fit perfectly, and I had to tell the guys that I had secretly got their measurements. It took a lot of discipline for us not to practice in our uniforms, but we saved them for the big day.

Rodney also provided a bag full of wood bats, which we loved more than the aluminum ones we had been using. He worked out with us, pitched to us, and by the end of the week we were ready. More and more parents and even sportswriters started visiting our little field, and everyone thought it was funny that a home run to left was two hundred and fifty feet into Mrs. Ferguson's creek.

11

The Big Game

T he day of the game, we went over to the Little League field to watch our opponents play. They won 5-1 on a one-hitter by their ace pitcher. They hit well and played without errors. We were worried, but we knew at least that we wouldn't be facing their best pitcher that afternoon.

When we arrived at our own field, all decked out in our uniforms, we were so nervous that we could hardly concentrate on warming up. None of us had played in a real game before, though we always gave each other pretty good competition.

We had nowhere to sit, of course, but more than a hundred people stood around or sat in the grass. Our opponents, whose Little League uniforms said "Bechtel's Drug Store" on them, arrived in their play clothes because they weren't allowed to wear their uniforms.

Suddenly they were the ones who looked scared. Here they thought they were just going to play a bunch of farm boys in a field somewhere, and they find a complete team in uniform, on a pretty nice field, lines chalked, and umpires in place.

Rodney and I had worked out our lineup the night before, and he had to sit with the other spectators during the game. That was all part of the deal. No coaching. I submitted our lineup to the umpire. Brent would lead off and play second.

Bugsy hit second and would play short. I would pitch and bat third. Jimmy caught and hit clean up. Toby would be at first batting fifth, Loren sixth in left, Ryan seventh in center, Cory eighth at third base, and Derek ninth in right field.

Derek was our secret weapon. Usually you expect the ninth hitter to be the weakest, especially if he's not a great fielder, which Derek wasn't. But he was the third best hitter on our team. We put him last to see if they would relax when he was up, especially if they were as good as they looked, and we hadn't had a hit yet.

In the first inning I was nervous and wild and walked three batters. I kept looking at my mom and my sisters. The girls were playing and not watching, but for this game Mom was watching me. I tried harder than ever, but the hitters looked so big and professional that I was afraid to lay the ball in there.

With two out and the bases loaded I slowed my pitches a little and decided that if they were going to beat me, they would have to do it by hitting not walking. The next pitch was a little too good and their number six hitter, Gary Stephenson, got pretty good wood on it.

He drove it deep to right field, but it was catchable. Derek drifted back and over near the foul line and missed it. It bounced fair and skipped into foul territory. By the time he tracked it down, I was backing up Jimmy and we were waiting for the throw from Toby, the cutoff man.

If his throw hadn't been perfect, it would have been a grand slam homer. Three runs scored ahead of Stephenson, but he was out on a close play at the plate. We were finally out of the inning.

Our first two hitters struck out and didn't look good, and I could see by the looks in their eyes that they had never faced pitching like this before. Both Brent and Bugsy whispered to me on their way back to the bench. "Make him throw strikes."

I had noticed that they struck out on bad pitches, so even though the pitcher was strong and fast, he didn't have good control, same as I hadn't. I waited until he had a two ball, no strike count on me and then laid down a bunt.

The catcher's throw actually had me beat at first base, but it flew over the first baseman's head, and I wound up on second. Jimmy drove a shot that would have easily got between the left and center fielders, but the shortstop leaped and caught it on the rise. I would have scored, but we went into the top of the second down 3-0.

For some reason, I felt I had lost all my jitters when I was warming up before the second inning. My fastball felt alive, and there was good movement on the ball. It was tailing up and in just the way it was supposed to.

For my last two warmup pitches, I tried one that started over the plate and slid inside and one that started outside and sailed over the plate. For the next three innings, I alternated those two pitches, baffling the hitters, striking out five, getting two on pop outs, one on a roller back to the mound, and another on a bunt to third.

Meanwhile, Jimmy hit a homer into the creek with Bugsy on second—he had walked. Going into the top of the fifth inning, we trailed 3 to 2. I still felt strong but may have been getting tired or over-confident because I lost a little control again.

I had fallen behind the first hitter three and O when I heard the shout of encouragement that sounded so familiar. "C'mon, Dal! You can do it!" It wasn't Rodney. It wasn't Mr. Calabresi. It had come from over by my mother. I stole a glance.

It was Dad! My dad had come back just for this game! I hadn't seen him for weeks, but there he was, looking big and strong and tanned and happy as ever. He had a fist raised in the air and repeated his shout. "You can do it!"

And I believed I could. I was so excited that I knew I had to keep the ball down because my extra strength would make it sail even more. The next pitch started low and away and tailed right across the plate.

I threw harder and faster and with more confidence than

81

I ever dreamed I'd have. Between innings I ran and jumped into my dad's arms, and he hugged me tight.

"You gotta beat these guys."

I smiled. "We will."

With two out in the bottom of the fifth I swung late on a good fastball and hit a ground ball that skipped inside the first baseman and into right field, hugging the line. I didn't realize how hard I'd hit until I rounded first and saw that it had got past the right fielder too.

I chugged to third and saw the whole team waving me toward home. I stumbled and fell and rolled across the plate, but I beat the throw and we were tied, 3-3. I knew then that I could not allow one more run.

In the sixth, seventh, and eighth innings, I retired every batter, three of them on strikes. But we weren't hitting either. It was getting dark by then, and the umpires announced that the ninth would be the last inning.

In the top half I was tired. I walked a batter, struck out the next, and walked the next. Jimmy trotted out. "Don't worry about losing your streak. Let's get 'em."

"What streak?"

"You didn't know?"

"No."

"Since that triple in the first, you had gotten twenty-one hitters out in a row. You've got a one-hitter with thirteen strikeouts against one of the best Little Leagues teams in Park City."

I shook my head. "Yeah, and five walks."

"Forget those and get these guys!"

A perfect double play from Bugsy to Brent to Toby ended the threat, and now the game was ours to win or tie. Derek almost made us geniuses by leading off the bottom of the ninth with a drive to center that could have won the game.

Their center fielder chased it down though, and they all looked pretty relieved. Brent then walked, and Bugsy was safe trying for a sacrifice bunt. They muffed the play, and we had men on second and third and one out with me at the plate.

82

I admit I was nervous. I wanted a hit so bad I could taste it. But they didn't want to pitch to me. I had been hitting fairly well and had driven the left fielder back about two hundred feet once, so they walked me intentionally.

With the bases loaded and only one out, we just knew the game had to be ours. Especially with Jimmy Calabresi up. But he was robbed again. He smashed a line drive down the third baseline so hard that the fielder was knocked on his back when he caught it.

All three runners had to dive back to our bases, and if the third baseman hadn't been knocked down, he could have doubled any one of us off easily to end the game in a tie.

Now it was up to Toby, our husky first baseman. He hadn't had a hit all day, but he hadn't struck out either. I knew he'd get wood on the ball. First he fell behind O and one on a good curve.

The next three pitches were also curves, and they all missed outside. I yelled to him at the top of my voice. "Take the walk! Take the walk! We'll take it any way we can get it."

But that wasn't Toby. He didn't want to win it the easy way. He knew the pitcher wanted to do anything but walk in the winning run, so Toby dug in and waited for the perfect pitch. Boy, was he ready.

The ball came in about waist high, fast and straight. And Toby teed off. He drove the ball far and deep to left, and I started jumping. I couldn't see any way anyone could get to that ball. The left fielder turned and raced straight back, head down, not even looking at the ball.

It had him beat. I saw it going past him, still several feet over his head. The center fielder, a real gazelle, streaked over from his position, but the ball looked farther than Jimmy had hit his.

The center fielder flashed past the left fielder and leaped high in the air, stretching his body out flat over the creek. The ball appeared to drop into his glove just before he splashed into the water with a huge gush.

The infield umpire was on his way out there on the dead run, and every eye in the place was on the spot in the water where he went under. He came up hatless and shaking the water from his head, holding his drenched glove aloft. He reached into it with his bare hand and produced the ball.

And the umpire signaled the third out.

Epilogue

We wanted to win, but short of that, the game couldn't have ended any better for us. We had tied a great Little League team, had played well, and impressed everyone.

Both teams wanted to play off the tie, but we had agreed to play until dark, and whatever happened would happen. The write-up in the paper got us lots of popularity, and we challenged any other Little League team in town to take us on.

By the end of the summer, we had played eight teams. We won three games, lost four, and tied one. The best thing that came of it was that the Baker Street Sports Club was something to reckon with. Before we knew it the weather got cold, and we started thinking about finding a place to play basketball.